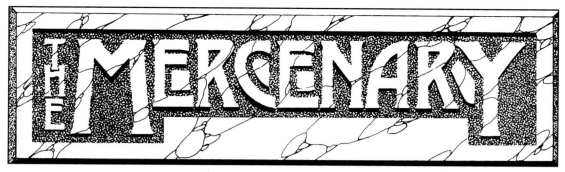

THE MERCENARY

YEAR 1000: THE END OF THE WORLD
V. SEGRELLES

NBM

We have over 200 graphic novels
available. Ask for our color catalog:
NBM
185 Madison Ave., Ste. 1504
New York, NY 10016

ISBN 1-56163-161-2
©1995 Vicente Segrelles
©1996 NBM for the English translation
Translation by Robert Legault
Printed in Hong Kong

NANTIER · BEALL · MINOUSTCHINE
Publishing inc.
new york

'THIS REFERS TO MILLENARIANISM, A CHRISTIAN DOCTRINE THAT PREDICTED THE END OF THE WORLD AND THE FINAL JUDGMENT IN THE YEAR ONE THOUSAND.

REALLY, MASTER, YOU SHOULDN'T GO. YOU KNOW YOU ALWAYS COME BACK ALL DEPRESSED.

I HAVE NEVER MISSED THE APPOINTED DATE, AND I CERTAINLY WON'T MISS IT IF IT'S MY LAST CHANCE.

HE WON'T COME. HE'S NEVER COME. TOO MUCH TIME HAS PASSED...HE'S DEAD.

HOPE IS THE LAST THING ONE LOSES.

I DON'T UNDERSTAND. WHO ARE THEY TALKING ABOUT?

BE CAREFUL WITH HIM. HE ACTS STRONG, BUT HE'S VERY OLD

I'M FULLY AWARE OF WHAT I HAVE TO DO: GO FOR A RIDE WITH THE OLD MAN AND DON'T ASK QUESTIONS.

AND WHY ARE YOU BEING SO RUDE NOW?

I'VE BEEN WITH YOU A LONG TIME, AND I'VE SHOWN YOU I'M FAITHFUL AND LOYAL. I'M SICK OF BEING THE LAST ONE TO FIND THINGS OUT.

2

WHAT ARE YOU GRIPING ABOUT? WE'VE KEPT YOU IN BLISSFUL IGNORANCE, AND WE GIVE YOU THREE YEARS TO GET WHAT YOU CAN OUT OF THE LIFE YOU HAVE LEFT.

GIVE ME A BREAK! THIS WILL BE MY LAST TRIP TO THE CRATER. I DON'T LIKE NOT BEING TRUSTED.

YOU'RE A FOOL. YOU NEVER KNOW WHAT YOU'VE GOT TILL YOU LOSE IT. ANYWAY, THERE'S STILL TIME FOR YOU TO REFUSE THE MISSION.

MERCENARY, YOU'RE BEING UNJUST. NANTAY HAS INSISTED THAT IT BE YOU WHO ACCOMPANIES ME. YOU'RE GOING TO BE PRESENT AT A PHENOMENON ALMOST NO ONE IN THIS WORLD HAS SEEN. YOU SHOULD FEEL PRIVILEGED.

YOU DECIDE. BUT HURRY, IT'S TIME TO LEAVE.

3

HERE'S A GOOD PLACE TO SPEND THE NIGHT.

MASTER...IT'S HARD TO BELIEVE WE ONLY HAVE THREE YEARS LEFT.

THE SAD THING IS THAT IT COULD HAVE BEEN AVOIDED, BUT IT WASN'T. FATE DEALT A TOUGH HAND...UNLESS SOMETHING'S HAPPENED...

THEN...THERE'S STILL SOME HOPE?

I DON'T THINK...PERHAPS THIS TRIP WILL MAKE IT CLEAR...I STILL HAVE FAITH.

FAITH IN WHAT, MASTER? BELIEVING IS GOOD; UNDERSTANDING IS BETTER.

UNDERSTANDING...UP THERE IN THE SKY, IN SPACE, THERE ARE MANY PHENOMENA WE DON'T UNDERSTAND. BUT THE CATASTROPHE THAT'S COMING HAS A SIMPLE EXPLANATION: TWO PLANETS ARE GOING TO COLLIDE. AND I DON'T KNOW WHY I STILL BELIEVE, AGAINST ALL LOGIC, THAT IT WON'T HAPPEN.

4

BRING ME THE WATCH. IT CAN'T BE LONG NOW.

THE ANIMALS ARE VERY NERVOUS. AND I MUST CONFESS I'VE GOT THE CREEPS, ALSO.

MAGNETIC FIELD ALTERATION. THAT IRON ARMOR CAN AFFECT YOU A LOT. THE PROCESS IS NOW BEGINNING.

NOW YOU'LL SEE HOW THE OUTER ATMOSPHERE OF ANOTHER PLANET INTERACTS WITH OURS...THEY'RE JUST JUST RUBBING THE EDGES.

COME ON, MASTER, THAT CAN'T BE.

WELL, IT IS. IT HAS HAPPENED EVERY THREE YEARS IN AN EXACT CYCLE, AND IT IS WHAT WILL CAUSE THE END OF TWO WORLDS THE NEXT TIME AROUND.

WHAT WE'LL SEE IS RELATED TO THE INFINITE. BUT ALSO TO THE SMALLEST, TO INTERATOMIC SPACE. THEY ARE TWO PLANETS THAT ROTATE IN A DISTINCT DIMENSION.

I'D PREFER TO HAVE FAITH...BECAUSE I DON'T GET IT!

YES, IT'S BETTER. NOW IT'S TIME. ARNOLD'S INVENTIONS ALWAYS WORK.

THERE IT IS! RIGHT ON TIME, LIKE THE SUNRISE ITSELF.

NOW THE CONTACT BEGINS. IT LASTS TWO DAYS, BUT THERE ARE ONLY LIGHTS AT THE BEGINNING AND THE END.

HOLY GOD...LET'S GET UNDER COVER, QUICK!

BE CALM, MERCENARY. WE'RE SAFE HERE. I'VE COME HERE MANY TIMES, AND I'M STILL HERE. YOU MUST ONLY WATCH OUT FOR THE LAST LIGHT, THE GREEN, WHICH IS ERRATIC. YOU NEVER KNOW WHERE IT WILL COME. IT'S VERY DANGEROUS; IF IT TOUCHES YOU, YOU'RE GONE.

DEMONS IN HELL! I'M ALIVE!

IT CAN'T BE!

MASTER, THAT WAS QUITE A BLAZE. IT SEEMS I'VE SURVIVED THE GREEN LIGHT...WELL, YOU KNOW, OLD SOLDIERS NEVER DIE...

EVEN THOUGH THEY CAN GET A BIT TOASTED...

BUT...YOU AREN'T THE LAMA...

≶EXCUSE ME, I DON'T UNDER-STAND WHAT YOU'RE SAYING.≶

I KNOW THAT LANGUAGE... WHERE THE DEVIL AM I?

≶YOU CAN SPEAK TO ME IN YOUR LAN-GUAGE, I UNDERSTAND YOU PERFECTLY.≶

OH, THANK YOU, THANK YOU. COME INTO MY HOUSE.

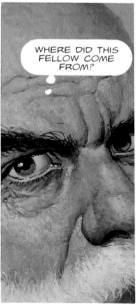

WHERE DID THIS FELLOW COME FROM?

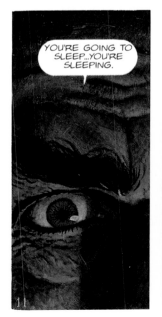

THE ARMOR IS OF PURE IRON...ALMOST WITHOUT CARBON...AND VERY MAGNETIZED.

EVEN THOUGH THE ARMOR MAY HAVE PROVIDED A PROTECTIVE COVER, HE'S FLESH AND BLOOD. IT CAN'T BE THAT EASY.

NOW YOU WILL TELL WHO YOU ARE AND HOW YOU WERE ABLE TO PASS TO THIS SIDE WITHOUT DISINTEGRATING. SPEAK CLEARLY AND IN MY LANGUAGE.

THEY CALL ME THE MERCENARY. I'M IN CHARGE OF SECURITY AT THE MONASTERY OF THE CRATER...I DON'T UNDER-STAND..."PASSING TO THIS SIDE"?...THE GREEN LIGHT! I'VE GOT TO FLEE THE GREEN LIGHT!

GREAT SATAN! HE KNOWS NOTHING. EACH TIME I UNDER-STAND LESS. IT WAS A DAMNED CHANCE OCCURRENCE. AND IT HAPPENED..HOW? THAT ARMOR ISN'T ENOUGH

TELL ME--SOMETIME WERE YOU EXPOSED TO A BIG BLACK BALL IN A LUMINOUS STATE?*

YES, IT WAS HUGE.

A THOUSAND GODS..PERHAPS HE'S PROTECTED TO PASS THROUGH BOTH STATES, AND I'M HERE, STRUGGLING WITH AN INSULATION THAT CAN ONLY WITHSTAND ONE.

*SEE THE MERCENARY'S STORY "THE BLACK GLOBE."

WAKE UP.

EXPLANATION...SOMEONE HAS TO GIVE ME AN EXPLANATION. ALL I KNOW IS THAT I WAS CAUGHT IN A GREEN LIGHT AND ENDED UP SOMEWHERE ELSE...MAYBE I'M DEAD.

YOU ARE NOT DEAD, YOU ARE JUST ON A DIFFERENT PLANET.

THAT CAN'T BE!

I KNOW IT IS HARD FOR YOU TO UNDERSTAND. YOU DO NOT COME FROM A VERY ADVANCED CIVILIZATION. COME, I WILL TRY TO EXPLAIN.

WE LIVE ON TWO PLANETS THAT SHARE ALMOST THE SAME PLACE IN SPACE, WITHOUT SEEING EACH OTHER...

THE TWO PLANETS FOLLOW FIXED ORBITS THAT COINCIDE. WHAT'S MORE, OUR SUN IS NEXT TO YOURS. THUS IT HAS BEEN SINCE THE BEGINNING OF TIME. THE LIGHTS YOU'VE SEEN WERE ALL THAT GAVE IT AWAY.

UNFORTUNATELY, A RANDOM COMET WILL SLIGHTLY CHANGE OUR ORBIT, AND AT OUR NEXT ENCOUNTER, WITHIN THREE YEARS, IT WILL NOT BE A LIGHT TOUCH BUT A HEAD-ON COLLISION, WHICH WILL CAUSE THE END OF TWO WORLDS.

THAT MAKES NO SENSE, IF WE OCCUPY THE SAME SPACE, WE'LL CROSS, AND THAT'S ALL.

NO, BECAUSE THE CORE OF THIS PLANET IS AN ENORMOUS BLACK BALL OF HIGH-DENSITY COSMIC DEBRIS. THEY CANNOT CROSS; THEY WILL EXPLODE...LIKE THIS.

14

NO, BELOW IT IS ONLY 5,000 METERS TO SEA LEVEL-- A HORRID DEPTH FULL OF DEAD BODIES.

HELL! LET'S GO SEE THIS WHITE SHELL.

LET US SEE IF THIS APPARATUS STILL WORKS...

COME, GET IN. DO NOT BE AFRAID, IT WILL NOT BITE YOU.

INCREDIBLE! IF ARNOLD COULD SEE THIS...

I WARN YOU, IT IS INDESTRUC-TIBLE. I HAVE BEEN UNABLE TO BREAK IT. AND BESIDES, EVEN IF YOU DID IT, YOU WOULD FALL INTO THE ABYSS.

THE ABYSS COULD BE AN ADVANTAGE...

IT'S VERY HARD. ONLY A TREMEN-DOUS BLOW WILL BREAK IT.

I HAVE THE SOLUTION.

YOU ARE A RESOURCEFUL MAN.

IF WE MANAGE TO MAKE A HOLE, CAN WE MAKE IT TO THE CENTER AND BACK IN TWO DAYS?

I SUPPOSE SO...

I HOPE YOU SUPPOSE RIGHT. DO YOU HAVE GUN-POWDER?

GUNPOWDER?

15

BOOMM...

...OOUMMM...

CRAKMM...

...NO HOLE ...IT DIDN'T BREAK...

ONLY CRACKS.

YES, BUT THEY'RE GOOD-SIZED CRACKS.

I FEEL A SLIGHT DRAFT. DOES IT FREEZE HERE AT NIGHT?

OH YES

LET'S PUT WATER AND SEALANT IN THE CRACKS. WITH LUCK, WE'LL HAVE A HOLE TOMORROW.

17

WARRIOR, WAKE UP!!

WHAT'S THE MATTER? HAS THE HOLE OPENED UP?

NO, THE "OTHERS" ARE HERE. YOU MUST HIDE. HURRY!

18

BUT DIDN'T YOU SAY YOU WERE HERE ALONE?

YES, YES, THE ONLY HUMAN LEFT. BUT THERE ARE THE "OTHERS," FROM THE HEIGHTS. THEY'RE DIFFERENT...AND DANGEROUS. MOVE, QUICKLY!

DON'T STRAIN YOURSELF, KAY

SPAAN, LOOK AND SEE IF YOU FIND ANYONE ELSE AROUND...

I'M WAITING FOR A GOOD EXPLANATION OF WHO THIS MAN IS.

HE IS MY NEW ASSISTANT. WITH HIM, I CAN PRODUCE MORE INSULANT FOR YOU. HE IS AN EXPERT.

IDIOT! DO YOU TAKE ME FOR A FOOL? YOU BROUGHT HIM HERE TO HELP YOU ESCAPE, WHO KNOWS HOW.

HEY, UGLY! YOU CAN'T TREAT AN OLD MAN LIKE THAT!

I SEE YOUR "EXPERT ASSISTANT" DOESN'T KNOW THE RULES OF THE GAME.

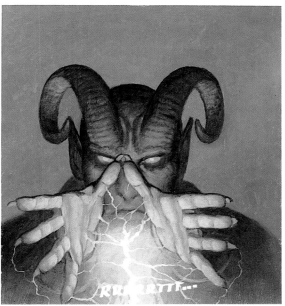

RRRRRTTT...

19

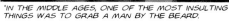

'IN THE MIDDLE AGES, ONE OF THE MOST INSULTING THINGS WAS TO GRAB A MAN BY THE BEARD.

AH!

W-WHAT... THE HELL HAPPENED?

HE THREW AN ELECTRIC CURRENT AT YOU THE WAY SOME FISHES DO. IT'S ONLY FATAL IF HE IS REALLY ANGRY. BUT THE WOMAN IS THE MOST DANGEROUS ONE. NEVER LOOK IN HER EYES.

ARCADIUS, YOU ARE MAKING A MISTAKE. I MEAN NOT TO FLEE. REMEMBER, THE GREEN LIGHT PASSED AND I AM STILL HERE. I HAVE KEPT MY PART OF THE BARGAIN.

THIS WORLD IS CRAZY.

THAT MAKES SENSE. I BELIEVE YOU.

ARCADIUS, THERE'S NO ONE ELSE HERE, BUT LOOK...THIS HUMAN IS A WARRIOR.

YOU OLD RASCAL. A WARRIOR TO DEFEND YOU...FROM WHAT? WE FEED YOU, WE TAKE CARE OF YOU--AND YOU BETRAY US. YOU WILL BE RESPONSIBLE FOR HIS DEATH.

WAIT, DARLING. I THINK HE'D LOOK BETTER AS A STATUE OUT THERE.

ALL RIGHT. HE WILL BE A DETERRENT. BUT A STATUE OF A WARRIOR IS NO GOOD WITHOUT HIS PRECIOUS ARMOR. PUT IT ON HIM AND TIE HIM TO THE MILL-POST.

20

PLEASE, ARCADIUS, DON'T DO THIS, I ASSURE YOU HE IS MY ASSISTANT.

DON'T TOUCH ME, YOU OLD TRAITOR! BE GLAD I NEED YOU. YOU CAN'T LIE TO A SATYR WITHOUT BEING PUNISHED.

ARCADIUS, BE CAREFUL. YOU ALMOST KILLED HIM.

HE'S JUST UNCONSCIOUS.

HE'LL LIVE LONG ENOUGH TO FINISH THE INSU- LANT WE NEED FOR OUR ARK. I PROMISE YOU I'LL TAKE YOU TO EARTH AT THE NEXT CONJUNCTION.

WARRIOR, LOOK AT ME. I ORDER YOU.

CRAK! CRAAAAK... CREEAK.

ONE MOMENT, STHENO.* YOU TWO, SEE WHAT THAT NOISE IS.

YOU WON'T BELIEVE IT, ARCADIUS. THE WHITE SHELL IS CRACKING.

21

*STHENO WAS ONE OF THE THREE GORGONS, WHO WOULD TURN ANYONE WHO LOOKED INTO THEIR EYES INTO STONE.

IT'S A DAMNED TRICK! STHENO, FORGET THAT! LET'S GET OUT OF HERE!

ARCADIUS, STOP AND THINK...

THE ORACLE SAID IT WOULD HAPPEN! IF THE WHITE SHELL BREAKS, THERE WILL BE A GREAT HURRICANE THAT WILL KILL ANYONE WHO'S NEARBY.

GO! I'LL BE RIGHT BEHIND YOU.

ARCADIUS, YOU HAVE THE BRAIN OF A GOAT.

HASN'T IT OCCURRED TO YOU THAT IF THESE TWO HAVE COOKED UP THIS SCHEME, IT CAN'T BE THAT DANGEROUS?

SURE, BUT...WHAT IF THEY DIDN'T KNOW ABOUT THE ORACLE? IT'S BETTER TO LEAVE.

YOU TWO STAY HERE AND LET ME KNOW WHAT HAPPENS. WE'LL WAIT FOR YOU IN THE LOWER CAVES OF OLYMPUS.

THIS IS PERSONAL NOW. I'LL BE BACK TO TAKE CARE OF THOSE TWO LATER.

KRAKM

BY ZEUS! LET'S GO, QUICKLY!

THE ORACLE WAS RIGHT!

MERCENARY, I TOOK A LOOK AT THE HOLE. IT IS SMALL, BUT THE LIFTER WILL FIT THROUGH.

WHY DIDN'T YOU WAKE ME? I WOULD HAVE HELPED YOU.

NO NEED. I WENT OUT TIED TO THE CABLE. THE WIND IS WEAKER THAN I THOUGHT IT WOULD BE.

GREAT.

WE CAN DESCEND IN MY LIFTER, BUT I FEAR IT MAY NOT HAVE ENOUGH POWER TO GET US BACK UP.

OH! THAT SOUNDS *REAL* GOOD!

I AM SURE THAT DOWN THERE WE WILL FIND SOME WAY TO GET BACK UP...ANYWAY, WE'RE DEPENDING A LOT ON LUCK.

YES, YOU CAN'T WIN WITHOUT PLAYING THE GAME. I'LL PUT MY ARMOR ON.

NO, NO ARMOR. THERE'S STILL NO BREATHABLE AIR DOWN THERE.

IT FITS ME LIKE A GLOVE.

WE DON'T HAVE TOO MANY CYLINDERS OF OXYGEN, BUT THERE ARE A LOT STORED WHERE WE'RE GOING.

OK, HERE WE GO.

MY GOD, I'VE GOT THE ENGINE ON FULL AND I STILL CAN'T CONTROL IT.

24

DAMN IT, KAY! THAT HOLE IS AWFULLY SMALL!

WELL, YES, IT IS A LITTLE NARROW.

NARROW?! YOU'RE GONNA KILL US!!

CRAK!

WE JUST SNAPPED OFF A LANDING STRUT.

HOW COULD THIS DISASTER HAPPEN?

IT WAS AN ACCIDENT. ONE OF THE STOREHOUSES OF REFRIGER-ANT FOR THE SYSTEM WE WERE GOING TO USE TO DEFLECT THE PLANET EXPLODED.

THE SMOKE FROM THE FIRE FORMED A GAS SHELL AT AN ALTITUDE OF 5,000 METERS...SUDDENLY, SIX DAYS LATER, IT POLY-MERIZED AND FORMED THE WHITE SHELL. IT WAS A MATTER OF SECONDS...I'VE ANALYZED IT CAREFULLY. IT ABSORBED ALMOST ALL THE OXYGEN AND PART OF THE NITROGEN. THAT WAS TWENTY-ONE YEARS AGO...TWENTY-ONE YEARS OF SOLITUDE.

IN ALL THAT TIME YOU NEVER MAN-AGED TO PASS OVER?

THE FIRST TIMES I DIDN'T HAVE THE CAPSULE READY. THEN THERE WERE UNEX-PECTED VISITS, AND THE LAST TWO TIMES THE LIGHT DIDN'T PASS WHERE IT SHOULD HAVE.

IN THIS CITY WE SHOULD BE ABLE TO FIND AN "RPV."

A WHAT?

"RAPID POLICE VEHICLE." A VERY FAST SHIP.

THERE'S ONE. LET'S LAND.

TREAD CAREFULLY. THERE CAN'T BE ANY HIGHER ANIMALS, BUT THERE COULD BE INSECTS...BIG ONES.

THIS REMINDS ME OF A SUBMARINE VESSEL THAT MY FRIEND ARNOLD MADE.

SUBMARINE VESSEL? THOSE ARE BIG WORDS.

THIS CITY IS ATLANTIS. I WAS BORN HERE...

IT'S IMPRESSIVE.

YES, VERY OLD. A THOUSAND YEARS AGO AN EXPEDITION TO YOUR PLANET LEFT FROM HERE. THEY NEVER RETURNED. A RESCUE MISSION LEFT--SAME RESULT. SINCE THEN, IT HAS BEEN FORBIDDEN TO TRY.

NOT SO STRANGE. IN MY LAND THEY KILL AT THE DROP OF A HAT.

HERE ALL CRIME DISAPPEARED WHEN THEY LEGALIZED THE TRUTH SERUM...LET'S GO.

WHOOOOO!! HOLY COW!!

FOOOOOUM...

KAY, I'M PUZZLED. DOESN'T IT SEEM STRANGE THAT I KNOW YOUR LANGUAGE?

NOT ESPECIALLY. MY LANGUAGE IS VERY OLD, AND I THINK IT IS POSSIBLE IT IS KNOWN IN YOUR LAND. BEAR IN MIND THAT, UNTIL THE LIGHT CHANGED, THE "OTHERS" OFTEN CROSSED OVER. THEY'RE NOT SUBJECT TO OUR LIMITATIONS.

THOSE LIVING MYTHS DON'T COUNT. THEY'RE NOT REAL.

LET'S SEE...THE LAST TO CROSS OVER OFFICIALLY WERE SOME RELIGIOUS DISSIDENTS WHO BELIEVED WE COULD PASS THROUGH TO THE FIFTH DIMENSION AFTER DEATH. THEY WERE EXILED A THOUSAND YEARS AGO. A LITTLE LATER, THE LIGHT TURNED GREEN AND NO ONE ELSE COULD CROSS.

THE DEVIL YOU SAY! IT'S ALL FITTING TOGETHER. THOSE DISSIDENTS--DID THEY KNOW ABOUT THE FUTURE COLLISION OF THE PLANETS?

YES, IT HAD JUST BEEN DISCOVERED AND WAS A STATE SECRET. BACK THEN THERE WAS NO KNOWN WAY OF AVOIDING IT. THEY FOUND OUT AND MADE TOO MUCH TROUBLE...

YES, BUT I'M THINK-ING OF SOMEONE MORE RECENT...

MY BROTHER AND GRAND-DAUGHTER!

EXACTLY! I KNOW THEM!

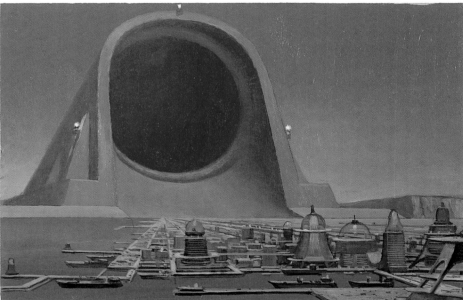

I HOPE THE CONTROL SYSTEMS STILL WORK.

THIS DEVICE RECOGNIZES THE CONVOLUTIONS OF THE BRAIN. NO ONE CAN FOOL IT.

YOU CAN'T ENTER. WAIT FOR ME HERE.

KAY, THE DOOR! SOMEONE'S THERE!

MY GOD!

SCARED THE HELL OUTTA ME, BONEHEAD!

HEAVENS ABOVE, THIS MUST BE PROFESSOR MENKENAY...THEY'RE ALL ENTOMBED HERE...I'LL NEVER KNOW HOW IT HAPPENED.

32

PLENTY OF ENERGY LEFT...LET'S SEE IF THE FUSION WAS PROGRAMMED...YES, ALL WE NEED TO DO NOW IS WAIT.

OK, THAT'S IT. LET'S PRAY THAT EVERY COMPONENT STILL WORKS AND HOPE THAT DAMNED COMET ARRIVES ON TIME.

IT'S HARD TO BREATHE. HOW IS YOUR OXYGEN?

BAD. I STARTED THE LAST CYLINDER A LITTLE WHILE AGO.

THERE SHOULD BE PLENTY MORE IN HERE.

EMPTY? IT CAN'T BE!

NOT ONE!

NOT ONE!! I DON'T UNDER-STAND...WELL, THERE'S STILL A PRESSURIZED ROOM WITH A RECHARGER. COME, QUICKLY!

FINISHED...NO... MORE...AIR...LEFT.

THIS...IS IT. WE'LL SEE...IF THE FIFTH... DIMEN...SION... REALLY...EXISTS...

SMOTHERED... AND...EATEN... NEVER THOUGHT...I'D... DIE...LIKE...THIS...

FLOUP!

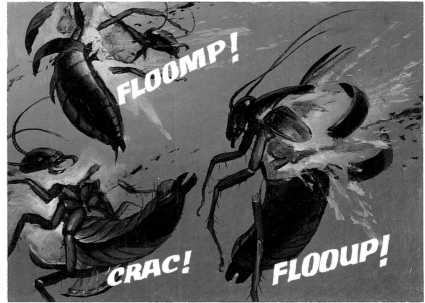

FLOOMP!

CRAC!

FLOOUP!

WHO'S BEEN MESSING IN MY STOREROOM?

PERK UP, I GAVE YOU A NEW CHARGE.

35

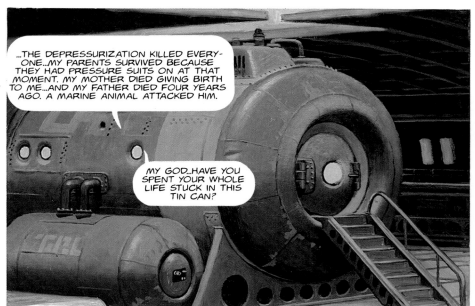

...THE DEPRESSURIZATION KILLED EVERYONE...MY PARENTS SURVIVED BECAUSE THEY HAD PRESSURE SUITS ON AT THAT MOMENT. MY MOTHER DIED GIVING BIRTH TO ME...AND MY FATHER DIED FOUR YEARS AGO. A MARINE ANIMAL ATTACKED HIM.

MY GOD...HAVE YOU SPENT YOUR WHOLE LIFE STUCK IN THIS TIN CAN?

NO WAY. THE WORLD IS MINE. I COME AND GO EVERYWHERE. FOOD, AIR, TRANSPORTATION, WATER...I'VE GOT IT ALL. THIS IS JUST MY GENERAL QUARTERS. MY HEART SKIPPED A BEAT WHEN I SAW YOUR LIGHTS, AND I CAME RIGHT AWAY.

THANK GOD YOU SAW US, NAN-KY. IF NOT, WE'D BE LIKE MY OLD FRIENDS IN THE CONTROL ROOM BY NOW.

YOU GOT IN THERE? THAT'S THE ONE PLACE I'VE NEVER BEEN ABLE TO ENTER.

MY FATHER WAS A TECHNICAL CONTRACTOR AND HE DIDN'T HAVE ACCESS TO THAT ROOM. BUT HE TOLD ME THAT IF ANYONE EVER MADE IT INSIDE, MAYBE THEY COULD STOP THE COLLISION. HE WAS CONVINCED THAT NO ONE HAD HAD TIME TO SHUT DOWN THE REACTOR.

THAT'S RIGHT. BUT THAT'S ALL TAKEN CARE OF. THERE WILL BE NO COLLISION.

THIS IS MY LUCKY DAY! THANK YOU, GOD!

NOT SO FAST. YOU CAN'T STAY HERE ALONE YOUR WHOLE LIFE, AND WE HAVE TO LEAVE THIS PLANET.

YOU HAVE TO LEAVE? YOU TOO, MERCENARY?

I'M AFRAID SO. THE TWO PLANETS WILL MEET FOR THE LAST TIME IN ABOUT TWELVE HOURS. WE DON'T HAVE MUCH TIME.

OH...WELL, ANYWAY, I'M NOT ALONE. MY FATHER TOLD ME BEFORE HE DIED: "KEEP SEARCHING, THERE MUST BE SOMEONE ELSE WHO MANAGED TO SURVIVE."

IF YOU HAVEN'T FOUND THEM BY NOW, TOO BAD...THE BEST THING YOU CAN DO IS GO WITH THE MERCENARY. I'LL STAY HERE, I AM AN OLD MAN.

LEAVE MY PLANET? ME? NO WAY. BESIDES, TAKE A LOOK AT THAT GAUGE: THE OXYGEN LEVEL IS INCREASING LITTLE BY LITTLE. THE DAY WILL COME WHEN I WON'T HAVE TO WEAR THIS SUIT.

IS THIS GAUGE WORKING?

OF COURSE.

OF COURSE. IT'S GOING STRAIGHT UP! SOMETHING'S HAPPENING OUT THERE.

FINALLY!

WHERE ARE YOU GOING? WAIT! WE DON'T KNOW...

THE GAUGE NEVER LIES. OXYGEN AND NITROGEN IN JUST THE RIGHT PROPORTION!

YES! IT WAS RIGHT! IT WORKS, IT WORKS!

SUN! SUN! HERE I AM! LET'S MEET AT LAST!

DADDY, I TOLD YOU THE DAY WOULD COME... I TOLD YOU.

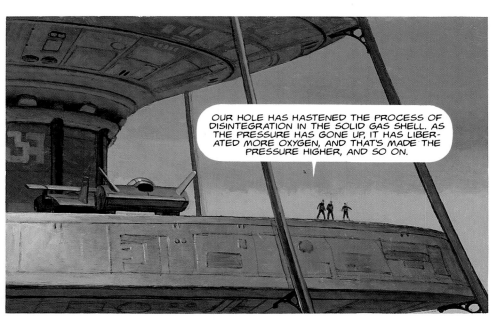

OUR HOLE HAS HASTENED THE PROCESS OF DISINTEGRATION IN THE SOLID GAS SHELL. AS THE PRESSURE HAS GONE UP, IT HAS LIBER-ATED MORE OXYGEN, AND THAT'S MADE THE PRESSURE HIGHER, AND SO ON.

DADDY, MOMMY, LOOK...I DID IT.

NOW IT DOESN'T MATTER TO ME IF I STAY HERE ALONE.

IT'LL ONLY TAKE A MOMENT. DON'T WORRY, YOU'LL GET BACK IN TIME. I KNOW HOW TO GET MAXIMUM PERFORMANCE FROM THIS "RPV."

WATCH FOR ANIMALS. TAKE MY MICROWAVE GUN; IT'S HOMEMADE, BUT IT WORKS JUST FINE. ALL YOU HAVE TO DO IS POINT AND PULL THE TRIGGER.

BUT...WHAT ARE YOU GOING TO DO?

THIS

THINK SHE KNOWS WHAT SHE'S DOING?

THAT LITTLE SAVAGE IS A BORN SURVIVOR. I DOUBT THERE'S ANYTHING SHE DOESN'T KNOW HOW TO DO.

FOR GOD'S SAKE-- SHE'S BEEN DOWN THERE A LONG TIME, AND I CAN'T SWIM.

I CAN. HELP ME TAKE OFF THIS SUIT.

INCREDIBLE. YOU'VE GOT TO TRY IT.

I WOULD LOVE TO, BUT WE DON'T HAVE TIME.

TRUST ME.

NOW YOU'RE REALLY GETTING CRAZY. IN MY COUNTRY NOBODY BATHES LIKE THAT OF THEIR OWN FREE WILL, AND NEVER TWICE IN A ROW. DRY YOURSELF OFF.

NAN-KY? SOUNDS ALMOST LIKE A GIRL I KNOW, NAMED NAN-TAY.

"NAN" IS A PREFIX THAT MEANS A YOUNG GIRL WHO'S NOT ENGAGED.

39

WE'RE ALMOST THERE. THAT CITY IS ATLANTIS. TURN EAST HERE.

THERE IT IS. WE'RE RIGHT ON TIME.

MERCENARY, THE FIRST THING YOU NEED TO DO IS PUT ON YOUR ARMOR. IT MAY SAVE YOUR LIFE. AND KY, YOU NEED TO DRESS WARMLY.

KY, YOU HAVE TO DECIDE. YOU'RE STUNNED BY ALL THAT'S HAPPENED, YOU HAVE TOO MUCH OF YOUR LIFE AHEAD OF YOU TO STAY HERE ALONE. YOU MUST GO WITH THE MERCENARY.

I DON'T KNOW WHAT TO DO...

HOW TOUCHING!!

41

43

HURRY, THE GREEN LIGHT IS ALMOST HERE.

THIS MUST BE IT.

WE'VE GOT TO GO!

MERCENARY, YOU'RE FREE TO GO BACK TO YOUR PLANET. DON'T DO THIS FOR ME...

I HAVE TO KEEP MY PROMISE. I'LL STAY WITH YOU.

BE CAREFUL. IF THE GREEN LIGHT TOUCHES US, WE'LL BE SPREAD OUT ALL OVER SPACE.

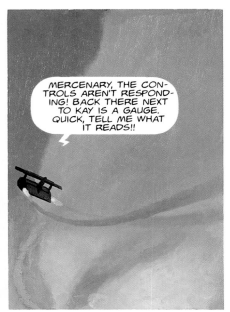

MERCENARY, THE CONTROLS AREN'T RESPONDING! BACK THERE NEXT TO KAY IS A GAUGE. QUICK, TELL ME WHAT IT READS!!

I DON'T LIKE PEOPLE DOING THINGS OUT OF OBLIGATION.

44

AND ANYWAY, I'M NOT HERE ALL ALONE. I'LL GO SEE WHO THIS ZEUS IS...

KY! FOR GOD'S SAKE! WHERE ARE YOU!!!